The Little Corn Seed

By

Sophie H. Nguyen

Once upon a time there was a little corn seed.

It was a lost seed, for a gust of wind had blown it across the land.

After days of traveling, the seed finally landed in a meadow.

But not just any meadow, but a corn plant meadow.

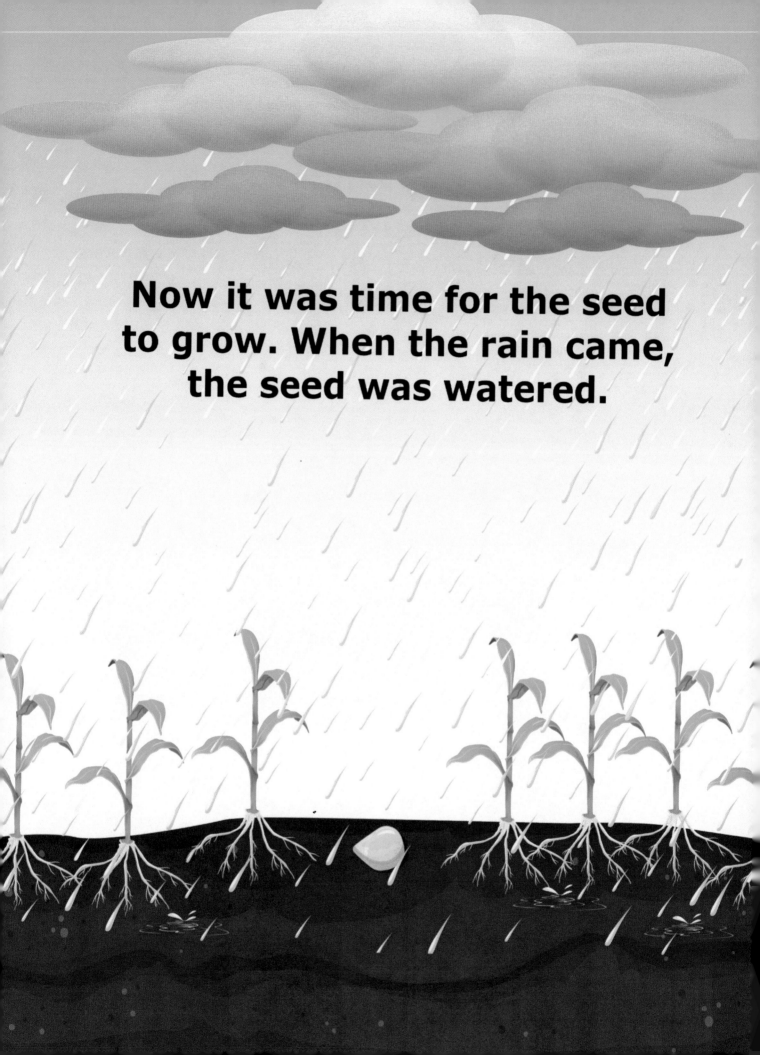

Now it was time for the seed
to grow. When the rain came,
the seed was watered.

And it grew stage,

by stage,

by stage.

Then when it was ready for pollination, a nibble bug came.

The nibble bug wanted to eat the plant, but the plant quietly asked the wind, "Can you help me?".

The corn plant was now an adult. It was the biggest corn plant in the meadow.

Now no bugs or animals could hurt the plant. Because if they did, the wind would blow them away.

Thank you, Wind.

The plant was finally ready for pollination. Then a heart butterfly came. It was the most beautiful butterfly ever.

The nearby village had a tradition of harvesting corn for their festival.

That person was a girl and she wanted to build a statue to honor the plant.

So she got to work. It took three whole days! But it was done.

It was the day of the corn festival. She decided to reveal the statue at the festival.

Time for the reveal. She pulled down the blanket and...

It was beautiful!!!

With all of the corn, they made many, many things. Corn pie, corn bread. You name it, they made it!

And that was the story of the corn seed.

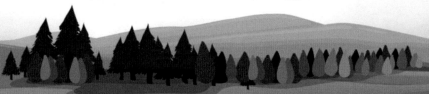

THE END

Dont forget to be a

CORNRIFIC

person!

The Little Corn Seed

by: Sophie Nguyen

Upon A Time there was a corn seed.

was a lost seed, for a gust wind has blown it across land.

r days of traviling the se y landed in a meadow.

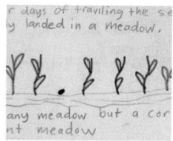

any meadow but a cor nt meadow

it was time for the see grow. When rain came it v ered.

ug wanted to eat the plant. the plant quietly ask the "can you help me?".

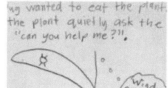

Wind, can you help me?

before you know it the w y the bug far across th d.

annh! save me

com plant was now an adu was the biggest in the adow.

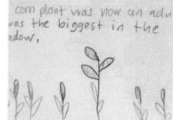

ne bug or animal hurts t nt. Because if they do th d blows them away.

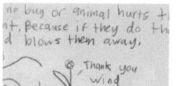

Thank you wind

no prob

plant was ready for polle n.

a heart butterfly came. the most beautiful one e

com plant was now an adu as the biggest in the dow.

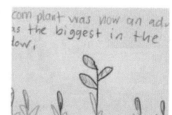

nearby village had a tra ion of havesting corn for ir festaval.

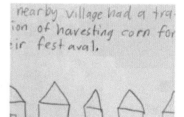

n they got there some one tted the giant corn plan

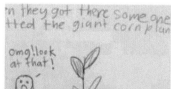

omg! look at that!

person was a girl and s ted to build a statue honor the plant.

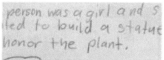

corn

she got to work. It e whale days! But It s done.

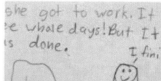

I fini

was the festival day. ided to reavel it at stival.

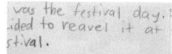

corn festival

for the reavel. She pul n the blanket and...

ool

so big

wow

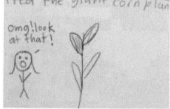

Corn

was beautiful!!!

all the corn they many things. Corn pie, bread, you name it!

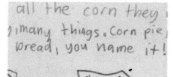

corn!

d that was the story corn seed.

rn!

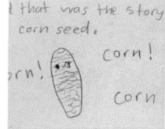

corn!

corn

The End.

t forget, be a ORNRIFIC rson!

Made in the USA
Las Vegas, NV
11 November 2023

80619571R00017